T0132331

A Long Journey to Paradise

Braylon's Island Adventure

By Mishka Veira Barnes, Ed.D.

Illustrated by John Floyd Jr

AuthorHouse™
1663 Liberty Drive
Bloomington, IN 47403
www.authorhouse.com
Phone: 1 (800) 839-8640

© 2019 Mishka Veira Barnes, Ed.D. All rights reserved.

No part of this book may be reproduced, stored in a retrieval system, or transmitted
by any means without the written permission of the author.

Published by AuthorHouse 04/30/2019

ISBN: 978-1-7283-0987-3 (sc)
ISBN: 978-1-7283-0988-0 (e)

Print information available on the last page.

Any people depicted in stock imagery provided by Getty Images are models,
and such images are being used for illustrative purposes only.
Certain stock imagery © Getty Images.

This book is printed on acid-free paper.

Because of the dynamic nature of the Internet, any web addresses or links contained in this book may have changed
since publication and may no longer be valid. The views expressed in this work are solely those of the author and do
not necessarily reflect the views of the publisher, and the publisher hereby disclaims any responsibility for them.

authorHOUSE®

For my parents, Cynthia and Samuel
Veira, who taught me how to be resilient.
For Braylon and Tomarcus,
thanks for the inspiration.

Braylon skipped down the stairs to the foyer. He looked up at me, smiled, and shouted, "Mommy, I am all dressed to go to St. Croix!" He felt proud. I explained, "You can't wear your swimwear on a plane. You will feel cold." He looked adorable! I tried not to giggle. Braylon replied, "Okay mommy, can you help me find something to wear?" We walked up to his room and I selected jeans and a long sleeve shirt.

We hopped into our SUV and drove off to the airport. The highway was congested, cars were everywhere. We rushed to the airport.

Braylon and I boarded the plane. He slept through the entire flight. Within 4 hours, we landed on the beautiful island of St. Croix. When we arrived, I woke him. He shouted with excitement, "Yippee, I can't wait to go to the beach!"

St Croix represents one of the islands of the United States Virgin Islands. The Virgin Islands consist of three islands, St. Croix, St. Thomas, and St. John. St. Croix is the largest island, at 84 square miles.

We picked up our SUV and we were on our way! Braylon rolled down the window to feel the cool breeze against his skin. "Next stop, the ice cream shop!" I shouted. At the ice cream shop, my son stared at the ice cream behind the counter. "Mommy," he asked, "What flavor should I get?" I replied, "I don't know... We have so much to choose from. Let's try banana." "Yummy," he shouted delightfully. I watched and giggled as the ice cream dripped down his face. "Mommy, this is delicious," he said. "It sure is, my son," I whispered softly.

The next day, Braylon was extremely excited. He yelled, "Mommy, today is beach day! We are going to Buck Island on a sailboat." Braylon and I packed our beach bag with snacks, like tamarind balls, fruit punch, bread, and salt fish.

We stepped onto the sailboat and zoomed over to the island. Braylon gazed at the beautiful white sandy beach. He yelled, "Can I build a sand castle?" I said, "Of course you can." He knelt down on the sand and began building the castle. Then, he jumped up and hopped onto his boogie board. He slid in and out of the water. Braylon played in the clear, turquoise water for hours.

Next, we hopped into our SUV and drove down to the Agricultural Fair. Braylon enjoyed petting the animals. He stared in amazement at the lazy pig as it rolled around in the mud. Then, he looked over at the next stall and said, "Look mommy, there's a goat." I said, "Yes dear, do you want to pet him?" Braylon reluctantly stretched out his hand to pet the goat. He giggled and said, "His fur is so soft."

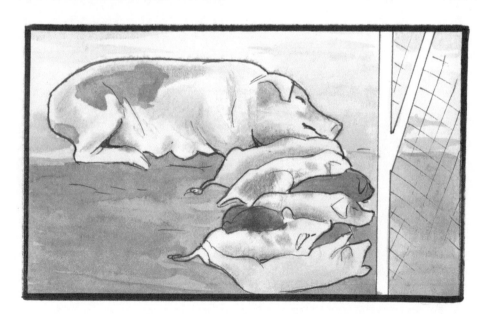

We strolled to another section of the fair and began tasting different island fruits like mango, soursop, sugar apple, and tamarind.

Next stop, an adventurous walk through the rainforest. We zoomed down to the town of Frederiksted. As soon as we arrived, we saw humongous trees. Braylon peered at the trees in amazement. The trees have been living for a long time. He said, "I wish we could climb them." We admired the natural habitat. Braylon stooped down, picked up a rock and said, "Mommy, can I have this rock?" I replied, "Put it in your pocket." He loves collecting rocks.

We watched as an iguana crossed our path. Then, we raced ahead of it.

We continued walking along a path covered by plenty of mango trees. I reached up and grabbed a mango. Braylon peeled it and began eating. The juice dripped down his face. Yummy!

It's a surprise! Braylon was asleep and I woke him. "Mommy, I'm tired," he said. It was 11:15 at night. I replied, "I know, my son, but I have a surprise for you. Get dressed." We jumped into our SUV and headed down to Sandy Point. When we arrived, the beach was closed because the leatherback sea turtles are emerging from their eggs! We received special permission to observe the emergence of the leatherback sea turtle hatchlings. I exclaimed, "Oh wow, it is amazing!" Braylon watched as the hatchlings emerged and scurried to the ocean. Magnificent! They were so small and delicate. "Can I touch one?" Braylon whispered. "No, not at all. Let's just watch them. We might scare and harm them," I said cautiously.

It was our final day on the island and we decided to cruise down to the Frederiksted Pier. We strolled around the beautiful pier. Then, we walked up to the shore and took off our shoes. Braylon and I stared into the transparent water and we saw huge turtles swimming.

Suddenly, we looked up and the sun was setting, it was a gorgeous sight. My son began to yawn. I reached down to pick him up. His feet dangled, he was exhausted. "Let's go home," I said.

It was time to return to the big city. We will miss our beautiful paradise island. It was a delightful experience! Braylon smiled and said, "Mommy, we have to return to Paradise!" I gazed at him in admiration and whispered in his ear, "Of course we will, my son, Of course we will!"

Printed in the United States
By Bookmasters